Will There Be

Watermelons

on Mars?

Debbie Manber Kupfer

Dedication

In memory of Yitzhak Rabin

Bring the day about

For it is not a dream.

And in all the city squares

Cheer for peace!

(*ShirLaShalom* by Yaakov Rotblit)

This story was created originally for the anthology,
Fauxpocalypse. It takes place the morning after everyone on Earth
believed the world was going to end . . . and then it didn't.

During the early 90s I lived in the Jerusalem neighborhood
of Nachlaot in a tiny apartment in Geva Street. This I shared with my
cat, Cici, and often hosted friends who would come and go. It was a
crazy time and was filled with . . .

Vodka and Watermelons

"Ouch... what...? Stop... let me sleep..."

Something was hitting my nose. Whatever it was I
wished it would go away. My head felt as if a gang of
marauding imps had forced their way through my ears and
now were attempting to pull out my brains piece by agonizing
piece. I groggily opened my eyes and tried to focus on the two
orange eyes staring back at me.

"Meooooow! Meooooow! Mrrrrrrrowwww!"

"Cici... STOP!"

I pushed my sandy and white feline out of my face
and attempted to sit up. It was desperately hot in the room and

my body was covered in sweat. I tried to get out of bed and instantly vomited on the floor.

"Cici, no, don't eat that... oh, what the hell..."

I stumbled across the room gingerly tiptoeing around the mess on the floor and went to the kitchen sink. I ran the water. Water, there was still water... wasn't there not supposed to be... but my fuzzy brain couldn't work out what there wasn't supposed to be. I grabbed a cup from the pile of dirty dishes in the sink, filled it from the tap, and gulped it down... That's better... well, not really, but it was a start.

I opened the refrigerator, and out rolled a watermelon onto my foot.

"Ouch! Son of a..."

The fridge had nothing in it but watermelons, and I'd no memory of how they got there. I look for milk, cheese, bread, anything. Nothing, nada, zilch, zippo. Nothing but watermelons. Oh, and vodka.

I didn't want watermelon, or vodka. Definitely not vodka.

There was a crash from the other room. Cici had knocked over an empty vodka bottle, one of the half a dozen dotted around the room like some chaotic abstract painting. I grabbed a dustpan and brush, and slowly began to clean up the mess. Shit, why was it so goddamn hot?

Cici watched me the whole time, supervising my work; she was a hard taskmaster that cat. As soon as I was done cleaning the mess, she came over and started nudging me with her nose.

"Hungry, eh? You and me both. Don't suppose you eat watermelon?"

I opened the closet in the kitchen, located the bag of dry cat food, and dumped some into a bowl from the sink. At least there was still cat food in the house, mainly because despite being hungry we were never *that* hungry.

Not that it was much of a 'house' – just one room, with a small kitchen attached, which opened onto a courtyard. Out in the courtyard were two smaller rooms; a bathroom with just a sink, and a shower with no shower curtain so that the water ran all the way out into the courtyard, and an outhouse with an old rusty toilet with a pull chain. It was one of the few hold outs in this rapidly gentrifying area of Nachlaot in the center of Jerusalem. Rent control, dirt cheap, landlord desperately wanted me out of here, especially as I'd stopped paying the rent months ago; there didn't seem to be any point what with the end of the world and all. Except that was yesterday... and the world was still here, and all I was left with was an opinionated kitty, watermelons, and vodka.

Oh... and Sasha. There were two mattresses on the floor of our room, plus a packing case that served as a table, an old scratched up wooden closet, and a bookshelf we managed to salvage from the rubbish one day.

From one of the mattresses came loud deep snoring worthy of a Neanderthal. Despite the heat Sasha had the cover over his head to block out the light. I knew it was pointless trying to wake him; he had probably drunk even more vodka than me last night. Strange really when you think that he'd been arguing for months that all the end of the world stuff was actually a bunch of crap.

I heard him muttering to himself in his sleep, "Nyet, nyet..."

I let Cici out into the courtyard, and went to the loo. We've been out of toilet paper for weeks now. We've been using torn up pieces of newspaper. Funny how the papers kept going even when the rest of the world was going to hell. Even the toilet seat was boiling hot that day. As I sat there I gazed at the headlines of last Friday's *Jerusalem Post,* "Less than a Week to Go".

All around the world people had been panicking, I knew. The scientists believed it was real this time; it really was

8

the end of the world. But not here in Jerusalem. Here in Jerusalem the majority of people believed they were safe, that God would somehow spare Jerusalem. So for the last few months, people from all over the globe had been flooding into Jerusalem, filling every corner of the city. They set up tents in the parks and parking lots. Some people were even living in the bus stops and on the street corners. Many rich Americans gave their life savings away just so that could come here and beg on the streets. Jerusalem, despite its small size, today had the highest density of population of any city on Earth.

And we hated them... us long-time Jerusalem residents, the secular holdouts from the time of Mayor Teddy Kolleck so many years before. We considered fleeing to Tel Aviv, Israel's party city, but why should we be forced to leave just because the world was going to end? Maybe... or maybe not...

God, I needed some tea. I came back inside and went back into the kitchen. I glanced over at Sasha. A few strands of long brown hair poked out from under the cover, apart from that, he was still deep in slumber snoring like a freight car. I envied his ability to sleep through anything – Ha, Ha, he could even sleep through the end of the world! I've never been that way, a cricket could chirp once at the other end of the courtyard and I'd be awake.

I boiled water on the stove in the old rusty green kettle. At least we still had gas; that was something, I suppose. I searched for some teabags and found a few Wissotzky Yellow Label. No sugar though. Sasha wouldn't like that when he finally got up. Me, I didn't care. I just needed some caffeine for this hangover headache. The Hangover After the End of the World... I smiled, that was probably pretty universal today. Last night those who weren't praying were drinking or fucking or both.

Some of my memory was beginning to come back from last night. I remembered meeting up with a bunch of Sasha's friends. We went to Supersol. The place was just kind of open. No one bothered turning up to work for the end of the world. Most of the shelves were bare, but we still managed to snag several bottles of vodka and some Bissli crispy onion rings.

We all walked to the park, and sat around in the children's playground and drank and talked. Shit, I couldn't remember what I talked about, probably told every one of them I loved them, or hated them, or... Well, maybe they wouldn't remember either.

The park was full of people, even at three in the morning. Well, it was always full of people these days, as many, many people slept there all the time. But last night no one was sleeping. No one wanted to miss the end of the world when it came. Everyone just kind of mulled around, looking for old friends, new friends, anyone to connect with. Sharing booze, cigarettes, dope. Couples disappearing into the bushes.

I vaguely remember there was one bloke (I can't remember his name). He said he was a plumber, that he was rich. Plumbers can charge anything they like. "Everyone needs to shit," he said. He tried to convince us all to become plumbers – hell, maybe I'll do that now... Suppose I've got to do something. We'll have to find a way to pay the rent if we want to stay here.

I drank my tea. It was too weak (Israeli tea is generally crap, but I ran out of the good stuff from England months ago). And now I was hungry, and I didn't want watermelon.

I grabbed an old faded T-shirt and a pair of shorts and sandals. I started to slowly gather the vodka bottles. Maybe if I took them to the market I could get enough money back for some bread. I glanced over at Sasha, but he was still dead to the world and probably would be for hours.

I walked out into the cobbled street. Geva Street looked exactly the same as it had yesterday. The sun was high in the sky, and I realized I had no idea what time it was... what day it was, even. For all I knew we could have slept for

11

twenty-four hours. For all I knew we could have slept for twenty-four years.

I heard raised voices from the upstairs flat opposite; the old couple going on at each other like they always did. Had they even known the world was supposed to end? I'm not sure they had a television. We only had a small black and white TV that barely got any stations. A friend had given it to us before she went on her world adventure, taking one of those 'last chance to see' trips. She had been an evangelical Christian. She'd believed in the end of days. We'd humored her.

So, what did we believe? Well... Sasha, as I said, thought it was all a load of crap, but that you might as well take advantage of it. So there was no need to work, plan, do anything much, when the rest of the world believed it wasn't going to be around for much longer. And me, well, I was an atheist Jew who bowed down to the shrine of science. It was scientists that said that this thing was going to hit the Earth, and there was nothing we could do to stop it... and scientists were right (usually).

Over the last months I watched the locals with scorn; those who believed they could pray their way out of this. Ha! I thought, you're finally going to understand when the day comes that there is no God, that all the stuff your Rebbes say is bullshit.

I made my way through the cobbled streets towards the market – Machaneh Yehuda. The supermarkets had been slowly dying over the last few weeks, but this market held on, though the stall holders had upped their prices and there had been shortages of some stuff, but not as bad as in other parts of the world. In London (where my parents still lived) I know there had been riots and lootings. Cities in the US had succumbed to gun violence. How would that all be resolved now that the world was still here?

Or was it? I had a strange thought. What if these folk around me in Jerusalem were actually right? What if the rest of the world was gone and this was all that was left, this one city, one oasis in the desert wilderness of Earth. Of course that couldn't be true, but what if? Suddenly as stupid as it sounded, I desperately needed to know that my crazy idea wasn't right.

I dragged my bag of bottles to the market, jostling my way through the crowds. There were so many people. Jerusalem had always been crowded, but not like this. It seemed that every dreg of humanity now lived in this city. Would they all stay now that the world was going on? Or would they crawl back to where they came from? If where they came from still existed, that is.

I weaved my way through the multitudes, the black-hats, the soldiers, the children sent out onto the streets to beg by their parents. That never used to happen here. We've always had beggars (that's a timeworn tradition in this ancient city), but not children before. Jerusalem had turned into a third world city; though perhaps, from what I'd seen on the television and read in the papers, the whole world was now the third world.

Finally, I pushed my way through to the bread guy, and offered him my empty vodka bottles. He stared at me with dark eyes, and silently counted the bottles before handing me a half a loaf of stale, two-day old bread.

"Toda rabah," I replied, "thank you."

Clutching the bread I made my way back to Geva Street. Maybe I'd convince Sasha to go on a trip; we could hitchhike to Eilat or something; go sleep on the beach for a while. I'd tell him the landlord would be after us for rent, now that the world hadn't ended. I wouldn't tell him my real reason for wanting to leave, that I needed to check if the outside world still existed. He would laugh at me, think I was being ridiculous.

I saw on the news a couple of nights ago that the government people were sleeping in Dimona these days, deep underground in the nuclear facility. Their scientists had told them that this was their best chance of survival. I wondered about that. Who did they think they'd be governing if everyone else was dead?

Cici met me in Geva Street. She wanted back inside to her food bowl. She meowed angrily at me: "Where have you been? Don't you know I've been starving here?" I opened the door and she glanced at her food bowl in disgust: "What, that old stuff?" Then she stalked over to Sasha still snoring on the mattress. Sasha turned in his sleep letting a cascade of long dirty brown hair overflow out of the cover. Cici took that as her cue to pounce. She leapt onto Sasha, digging her claws into him through the sheet.

"Hey... get lost... stupid cat!" But at least he was up now. I tore the bread in half and tossed some over to Sasha, then made more weak tea.

"Sashka, you want watermelon?"

"Sure Suzki. Where you get the bread?"

"Market... it's open."

"Still there... huh?" he said with a smile.

"Okay, go on, say it!"

"What?" he smiled innocently.

"You were right, the world didn't end. It's never going to end."

"Oh, I don't know about that. It will end eventually, but not when everyone says it will, never then."

I chewed for a while in silence, thinking about that.

"So what now?" I asked.

"Nothing," he said, "we just carry on."

"All right, have it your way," I answered, "but just tell me one thing; where did all the watermelon come from?"

In my interviews with the other Fauxpocalypse authors, I asked some of them what happened next in their stories. I've been thinking about that in relation to my own story "Vodka and Watermelons". What would Susie and Sasha do next?

During my time in Israel I spent a year living and working in the Arab village of Tira. During the first Gulf War I visited my friends in the village. There was a huge contrast between their attitude and that of my friends in Jerusalem. Whereas most of the Jerusalemites felt that they were safe from Saddam's scuds, the residents of Tira in no way felt immune. Many had sealed not only a single room, but their whole houses against what they believed was the very real possibility of a chemical attack from Iraq.

So here is another slice of watermelon...

Another Slice of Watermelon

A few hours later we're out on the street pushing through the hordes of people. I'd convinced Sasha that we needed to get out of the city for a while. Told him I figured the landlord would be after us for rent, now that the world hadn't ended. I hadn't told him my real reason for wanting to leave, that I needed to check that the outside world still existed. He would have laughed at me and thought I was being ridiculous...

We made our way down Jaffa Road, weaving through the multitudes, the soldiers, the black hats, the beggars. There were many, many people in the street, but while there are still a few cars, most were on foot. There had not been much petrol for months now. We passed the bus station. There were just a few buses running and the crowds were pushing and shoving to get on board. Sasha and I didn't have any money for the bus in any case. We walked on past the bus station and out of the city.

There was a junction there which we knew from many years of experience was the best place to hitch a ride out of Jerusalem. There were a few soldiers standing there with us and we knew already that any cars that stopped would take the soldiers first.

Still we had one advantage over the soldiers. We had nowhere in particular that we needed to go.

Out in the streets of Tira there was total silence. No one had emerged from their houses at all today. Na'ima sat on the stone wall outside her house. So it was still here – the world – she knew it would be despite everything her family and friends told her. Despite what they had told her at school. Despite what she'd seen on the TV screens, those hysterical voices from Al Jazeera blaming Israel and the Jews for all their troubles.

She had kept going to school even when most of her friends had stopped. Yesterday there had only been her and her teacher.

Na'ima was going to be a doctor; there would need those even more now. Now the world was still here. She wondered how long the rest of the village would sleep. When would they would wake up and realize they were all still here?

She looked down the street – a girl and a boy were walking towards her wearing shorts and T-shirts. Where had they come from? There had been no visitors to the village for months now.

We waited at that junction for nearly two hours, watching all of the soldiers disappear into vehicles. We had almost given up when a small truck stopped and asked where we wanted to go. We said we didn't care; wherever they were going was fine.

The guy driving the truck, Hamid, was trying to get back to his village. There was very little petrol left in the truck so this was unlikely. Still, he said, if Allah had saved the earth, surely another little miracle would be in order and maybe they'd find a petrol station along the way that still had petrol.

Many years before, I'd spent a year volunteering in the Arab village of Tira. I had been young and idealistic then, believed I could change the world – didn't realize that the world was not willing to change. It had been years since I'd been back to the village, yet today a few hours after the end of the world we found ourselves on the outskirts of Tira. Hamid's truck had broken down several hours before and we were on foot unable to find another ride.

As we walked into Tira I recognized the houses. It seemed like nothing had changed, yet it was eerily quiet. Where were all the people? I had friends in the village, or at least I used to, but I felt suddenly shy, unwilling to knock on a door, though we desperately needed water. I'd almost decided it was hopeless and was going to leave again when I saw the young girl in the distance sitting on the stone wall. Was she the only one left?

As we walked closer, she rose to meet us, smiling.

"Hello," said Na'ima, "Would you like some watermelon?"

Fast forward a number of years and Earth's technology has developed to the point that the first settlers are moving to Mars. For some this is a chance to start a new life free from the prejudice they suffered on Earth.

These are the new pioneers, the new chalutzim...

Chalutzim

Reuven shivered as he gazed out of the shuttle window. Mars – it was really happening. A new life, a new future away from those who judged. A fresh start.

He looked at Na'ima asleep by his side, strapped into her seat in the shuttle. The first commercial shuttle to Mars. Others had found sponsors willing to fund the first Mars settlers – the new Chalutzim. But they had sold everything they owned to make this trip.

His great-grandparents had arrived in Israel before the state was born. They had drained the swamps, caught malaria, and left the kibbutzim when materialism had taken over from idealism. Reuven had grown up in Tel Aviv and studied engineering in Bar Ilan University. It was there he had met Na'ima.

Na'ima had been the smartest girl in Tira. She had wanted to be a doctor, but had settled for studying to be an English teacher. At least it got her out of the village. Reuven had been attracted to her instantly – an electric pull of opposites – the young modern-orthodox Jew fresh out of five years of army service and the smart, ambitious Arab girl. It was forbidden, of course, which made it that much more delicious.

Neither of them told their families. There was no future in it after all. Jewish law dictated that identity was passed on through the mother. Muslims passed through the father's line. There was no civil marriage in Israel. They could do what others had done before them and go to Cyprus to marry; the government would at least recognize them then as married in that case. But still neither community would accept them, so they decided not to make the trip.

They thought that maybe it would be better to part, and they tried, but their attraction was too strong to break. Reuven had been called up for his yearly military service, and was caught up in the latest unrest in Gaza. He had spent six weeks policing the streets of Gaza City. Na'ima tried to ignore the news broadcasts of brutality on both sides, but had counted the days until Reuven came home to her. She had clung to him that night, desperate to have him inside her forever.

"Don't leave me," she whispered.

"Never," he promised.

They tried to live together in Tel Aviv, but the neighbors shunned them. Around this time, Na'ima discovered she was pregnant. The nurses in the clinic were a mix of Jews and Arabs, but they all looked at her in the same way, with pity and contempt in their eyes.

One morning, after four and a half months of pregnancy, Na'ima awoke with blood pooling between her thighs and a feeling of dread building inside her. "Just as well," the doctor muttered under his breath after confirming the miscarriage.

They moved to Tira. Maybe there they would be more accepted. They built a home on the outskirts of the village, and made friends with the two other mixed families that lived there, but no one else. Na'ima's family refused to acknowledge her presence.

Reuven traveled to nearby Kfar Sabah and worked in an electronics factory. Na'ima taught English in the village. The children whispered about her behind her back.

One day, a recruiter from the Technion Institute came to Reuven's factory. He left pamphlets strewn all over the facility. The pamphlets showed pictures of a stark red planet, barren, unspoiled. *Chalutzei Chadash,* said the banner – the New Pioneers.

Reuven's factory made high-end robotics. Robots would be crucial on Mars. Terraforming was underway, and Israel's Technion Institute now had a department devoted entirely to developing the technology necessary to make the vision of the Red Planet a reality.

Reuven was fascinated with Mars. He came home each night with more information and spent all his free time scouring the web, joining every chat room and Facebook group devoted to Mars.

Still, even with sponsorship from the Technion, it would be expensive. It would take everything they had to make the trip. Did they really want to leave everything behind?

Since Reuven had moved in with Na'ima, his family in Tel Aviv no longer took his calls.

"Your ancestors didn't survive pogroms and malaria for you to take up with a shiksa!" His father had said before he slammed down the phone.

Na'ima's family was not much better. Unlike his parents, they had known about her pregnancy, and had breathed a sigh of relief at the news of the miscarriage.

"There's no future in it, Na'ima. Jews and Arabs have been at war for centuries. Do you really think Allah would make an exception for you?"

Allah? Did Allah's power extend to Mars? Na'ima wondered. She glanced through the pamphlets Reuven had left around their home and began to dream. She dreamt of starting afresh in a strange red world, where no one would care if they were Muslim or Jew. Maybe if someone asked what she was, she could say Martian! She smiled at that. In her spare time, she took to reading old science-fiction novels. She poured over the pages of Ray Bradbury's *Martian Chronicles*, dreaming about the future that just might be.

There were no indigenous Martians of course. She knew that. So far there were only scientists and military. The next stage would require engineers to build the planet. Reuven would have plenty of work, plenty of distractions, but what would she do on Mars? Initially there would be no children, so there would be no one to teach.

She fancied herself as a writer, chronicling the new world – the new Martian Chronicles maybe? She longed for the solitude of her future life, marking the days off on the calendar. She still hadn't had the courage to tell her parents. They would blame Reuven, but Na'ima knew the truth, that she wanted this for herself. She needed to start over, and would fight to go even if Reuven gave up the idea.

Then came a problem. As they were not married, Na'ima would need a skill of her own to be accepted on the Mars project. Her family were farmers – strawberries and guava. Na'ima had grown up helping in the strawberry fields. She enjoyed working with soil and seed. Growing food would be important to the Mars project. Earth was too far away, so they would have to be self-sufficient from the start.

The little water that had been discovered on the Red Planet lay deep within its bowels. Part of the Technion group was devoted to agriculture, and Na'ima applied to the program to be trained. She held her breath. What if they didn't accept her? Would Reuven go without her? There was fire in his eyes these days when he talked about Mars. Na'ima would hate to see that fire extinguished.

They were interviewed both separately and together. At each stage they both feared they'd be rejected. Did they understand that there was no going back? The investment was too large to accept those who were not willing to spend the rest of their lives on Mars. If they were accepted into the program they would be leaving Earth forever. Yes, they understood. And their families, did they understand? Their families didn't care. The recruiter looked between the two of them and nodded.

That night, they discussed it and decided they should each try and visit their parents one last time.

Reuven only got as far as his front door. His father opened it and looked at him in contempt.

"What, have you left the shiksa?"

"No," said Reuven, simply.

"Then we have nothing to say."

"I'm going to Mars..." Reuven shouted as his father shut the door. He didn't know if his father heard him.

Na'ima's family thought it was a joke.

"Ha! You're running off to America. Send us a postcard from Disney World."

"It won't be any better there, you know? The Americans hate the Arabs and they'll despise you for being with a Jew. They talk about a melting pot, but that just means they want everyone to be the same. I wouldn't go to America if you paid me."

"I'm not going to America, I'm going to Mars."

"What? Where? What state is that in? Never heard of it. Nonsense! Hey, do you want some watermelon?"

It was hopeless. She walked home across the dirt road to their house that she'd shared with Reuven for the last four years. It started to rain and the streets morphed into mud baths. By the time she was home her shoes and pants were caked in mud.

"No," she decided, "I'm not going to miss this place."

Strangely enough, they did go to Florida as that was where the launch site was. They even spent a day in Disney World, and on a whim Na'ima sent a picture postcard to her parents back in Tira. It showed the newly-opened *Journey to Mars* ride in Epcot.

When she saw the shuttle her eyes met Reuven's. This was really it. Their new future started now. There was no going back. She squeezed Reuven's hand as they boarded the shuttle.

Reuven closed his eyes at the moment of lift-off, as the shuttle hurtled into space, breaking out of the Earth's atmosphere. But after the initial thrill of witnessing something that very few humans had, the days in space became tedious.

They studied, played games, read stories to each other, and got to know their fellow pioneers. They passed the time. Maybe someday the human race would invent warp speed like in those old TV shows, but not in Reuven's lifetime. The shuttle became their home in space. This he imagined is what Moses must have felt like as he wandered in the desert for forty years, not knowing if he would ever see the Promised Land.

Months after leaving Earth, their promised land was approaching. Very gently Reuven nudged Na'ima. She opened her chocolate-brown eyes and smiled at him. Beautiful, thought Reuven, catching his breath.

"It's time," he whispered.

Together they gazed out of the window in awe as the Red Planet came into view. The future was down there – their future. Reuven reached into the pocket of his spacesuit and pulled out a small square box. Now was the time.

"I promised you I would never leave you, Na'ima. Will you marry me?"

Na'ima accepted the ring and nodded. "I love you Reuven."

Five Years Later

A watermelon – just one. More would be wasteful with Mars' limited water supply. But Na'ima got permission to plant a single melon after her parents had sent the package – a peace offering from across the galaxy. It had taken months to arrive. A little packet and a scribbled note: *We believe you now.*

Nai'ma had cried and patted her growing stomach. Their child would be the first on Mars. The first of a new generation. The original Martian.

Acknowledgements

Several folk helped me on the road to creating this short collection. These include Schevus Osborne, Misha Burnett, Jeanne Felfe, and Larry Miller. Also a huge thank you to my daughter, Ronni Kupfer, for creating the cover and proofreading the stories.

The picture on the front cover was taken by my late father, Walter Manber. It gives me great pleasure to be able to use one of his photographs in this way. If you would like to see more of his work please visit The Photographic World of Walter Manber on Facebook, a page I set up in his memory.

"Vodka and Watermelons" was first published in the anthology, Fauxpocalypse. To read the rest of the stories pick up a copy on Amazon.

About the Author

Debbie grew up in the UK in the East London suburb of Barking. She has lived in Israel, New York, and North Carolina and somehow ended up in St. Louis, where she works as a writer and a freelance puzzle constructor of word puzzles and logic problems. She lives with her husband, two children, and a very opinionated feline. Her first novel, _P.A.W.S._, was published in June 2013 and the second book in the series, _Argentum_, was released in October 2014. In addition she has stories in several anthologies including _Fauxpocalypse_, _Shades of Fear_, _Darkly Never After_, and _Sins of The Past_. In February 2015 she published a book of logic puzzles, _Paws 4 Logic_, with her son Joey. She believes that with enough tea and dark chocolate you can achieve anything!

Connect with Debbie on her blogs, Paws 4 Thought and Paws 4 Puzzles.

Facebook, Twitter, Goodreads, or Amazon.

10954139R00023

Made in the USA
Monee, IL
04 September 2019